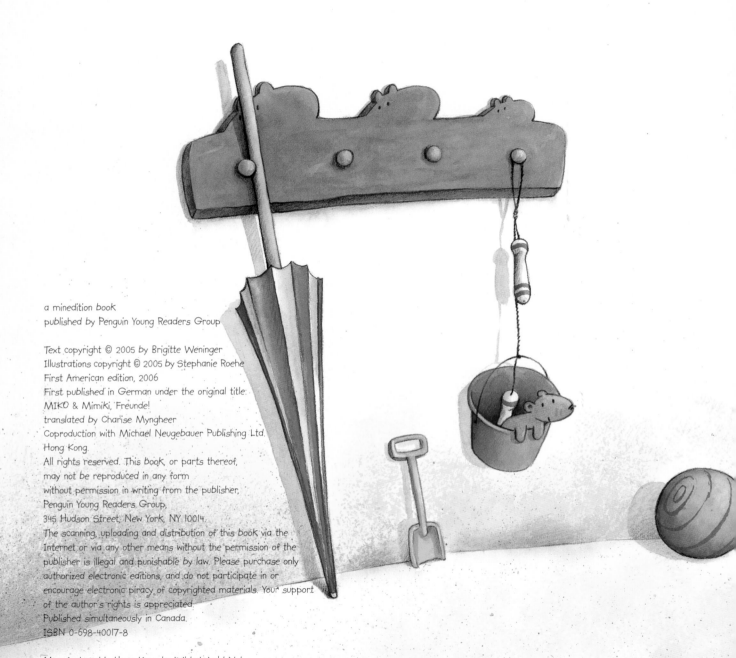

a minedition book
published by Penguin Young Readers Group

Text copyright © 2005 by Brigitte Weninger
Illustrations copyright © 2005 by Stephanie Roehe
First American edition, 2006
First published in German under the original title:
MIKO & Mimiki, Freunde!
translated by Charise Myngheer
Coproduction with Michael Neugebauer Publishing Ltd.
Hong Kong.

Published simultaneously in Canada.
ISBN 0-698-40017-8

Manufactured in Hong Kong by Wide World Ltd.
Typesetting in Kidprint MT.
Color separation by Fotoreproduzioni Grafiche, Verona, Italy.
Library of Congress Cataloging-in-Publication Data available upon request.

10 9 8 7 6 5 4 3 2 1
First Impression

Brigitte Weninger

MiKO Goes on Vacation

Illustrated by
Stephanie Roehe

minedition

"Good-bye house!" said Miko as he waved.
"We're going to the beach!"

When they arrived, Miko was surprised at how big the ocean was. "Wow! Look at all that water," said Miko. "Can we really swim here?"
"Of course you can," said Mom.
"You're going to love it!"

As Mom unloaded the car, Miko and Mimiki took a look around.
There were lots of fun things to do, but they didn't see anyone
they knew. Mimiki began to look nervous.
"Don't worry," said Miko "I won't leave you alone."

Miko put his swimsuit on,
and Mom rubbed sun block on his face.
"Are you ready to go swimming?"
she asked.

No!" answered Miko. "We can't go swimming without Mimiki.
What's he suppose to do?"
Mimiki will be fine by himself," said Mom. "Nothing
will happen to him."
No," argued Miko. "I won't leave him alone.
What if somebody takes him?"

"We can hide Mimiki in the beach bag,"
said Mom. "I'm leaving my wallet here too."
"No," said Miko. "We can get more money,
but there's only one Mimiki!"

"What should we do then?" asked Mom.
"I thought you wanted to go swimming and take
a boat ride."
"I know," said Miko. "But, Mimiki is my friend
and he should have fun too."
Miko looked around.
He still didn't see anyone he knew,
but he had an idea.

Mom watched Miko as he walked over to a little girl.
"Hi. My name is Miko, and this is my friend Mimiki.
My mom and I would like to swim. Can Mimiki play with you
while I'm gone?"
"Of course," answered the little girl. "My name is Mia."

"We'll take good care of him," said Mia's father.
Miko showed Mimiki exactly where he would be and promised
not to be gone long.

Then he ran back to his mom.

"Now, we can go swimming!" said Miko.

"That was a great idea!" said Mom.

And they raced into the water.

"Hmmmmm," said Miko smacking his lips. "The ocean tastes like french fries!"

Mom gave Miko a big wet kiss.

On his way back to Mimiki, Miko found a shell for Mia.
"Mimiki and I are going to build a sand castle.
You can help us if you want to!" said Miko.

Miko and Mia had fun building castles all afternoon.
"It's fun to swim and play at the beach," said Miko.
"But the best thing about going on vacation is
making new friends!"

For more information about MIKO & Mimiki and our other books, please visit our website: **www.minedition.com**